EARTHQUAKE!

Penn Mullin

Brayden

A HIGH ADVENTURE BOOK
High Noon Books
Novato, California

The author gratefully acknowledges the valuable assistance of Daniel Davidson, Emergency Medical Technician and pre-med student at the University of California, Berkley, in providing medical information for this book.

Cover Design and Illustrations: Herb Heidinger

International Standard Book Number: 0-87879-411-5

1 0 9
0 9 8 7 6 5 4

High Noon Books

20 Commercial Blvd.
Novato, California

Contents

Chapter 1

Job Time

"Hi. Gosh, what took you so long?" Jen called to her mother. "You're really late today." Jen was sitting on the couch watching TV.

Mrs. Young set two grocery bags on the kitchen table. She looked tired and hot.

"Please, Jen, will you turn down the TV? I've had a hard day. How about helping me put away these groceries?"

"Just wait a sec. Then I will. Julie just called. Everybody's going skating tonight. I'll need five dollars," Jen called to her mother.

"Another five dollars? I just gave you five yesterday. You can't keep this up, Jen," Mrs. Young said.

"Gosh, what's the big deal about five dollars? Didn't you get paid today?" Jen asked.

Mrs. Young walked over to the TV set and turned it off.

1

"OK, Jen. I've had enough. You think money's so easy to get? Well, try earning your own this summer. Get a job. No more of this sitting around and asking me for money."

Jen stared at her mother. Mom's just had a bad day, she thought. She'll cool down. She'll give me the money. No problem.

"Now come help me. And we can talk about a job for you." Jen's mother went into the kitchen. Jen followed her slowly. She looked up at the clock. She had to meet Julie in an hour. There wasn't much time. She had to get the money.

"I'm going to make us a tossed salad for supper," Mrs. Young said.

"Oh, I'm not hungry, Mom. I won't have time to eat," Jen said.

"Why not? Where are you going?" Mrs. Young took milk out of the grocery bag.

Jen was getting mad. She didn't need all this hassle.

"I'm going to the skating rink. Julie will lend me the money. She always has it. Her parents don't give her all this trouble," Jen said.

"I don't care what Julie's parents do. You're going to start earning your own money. I really mean it about a summer job," Mrs. Young said.

"It's not easy to get a job. All the good summer

jobs are already taken," Jen yelled at her mother. "And I don't want to sit in some dumb old office all day. No way."

"It doesn't have to be in an office. There are lots of other kinds of jobs. You'll see. Tonight we'll look through the want ads in the paper. Now, let's get going on this salad," Jen's mother said.

"I'm not hungry." Jen gave her mother an angry look. Then she marched down the hall to her room. She slammed the door shut behind her.

Chapter 2

Getting Started

Jen didn't come out of her room until morning. Her mother had left for work. She had left a note on the table.

Dear Jen,

Have some fresh strawberries. They're in the refrigerator.

I'll be home early today. We can go check out some jobs together. See you at three.

Love,

Mom

Jen stared at the note. Mom really means it, she thought. What a drag. Everybody will be at the pool all summer. And I'll be stuck at some dumb job. It isn't fair. Well, there probably aren't any jobs left anyway. Jen turned on the TV set and stretched out on the couch. She was still watching TV when Mrs. Young got home at three o'clock.

"I heard about some great jobs today, Jen! We could go check them out this afternoon," Mrs. Young said. "One of the jobs is at a day care center. They need extra help with the kids."

"No way. Kids crying all the time? Thanks but no thanks." Jen yawned and stretched.

"Well, another job is at Food World. Bagging groceries. Doing carryouts. Then there's one at the hospital," Mrs. Young said.

"The hospital?" Jen sat up on the couch. She liked TV shows about hospitals. But she couldn't stand the sight of blood.

"What kind of stuff would I be doing?" Jen asked.

"Just helping out the nurses. Taking newspapers and drinks to the patients. That kind of thing. How does that sound?"

"Sounds better than bagging groceries. A lot less work. But there's no way I'm going to be around any blood or anything like that," Jen said.

"Well, let's go on over to the hospital. We can find out more about the job," Mrs. Young said.

"Now? I don't know. I told Julie I might come over." Jen looked at her watch.

"I think now's a good time. The job might not be open tomorrow. Why don't you go put on your blue skirt? Then I'll drive you to the hospital," Mrs. Young said.

"Do I have to change? I'm OK like this." Jen stood up and smoothed down her jeans.

"It might be better to wear a skirt. It's important to look your best when you're asking about a job," Jen's mother said gently.

"OK. OK. But this is really stupid." Jen stomped off to her room.

Half an hour later Mrs. Young and Jen drove into the parking lot of Clayton Hospital. It was a small hospital with only thirty beds.

Jen had a strange tight feeling in her chest as she got out of the car. Who would she talk to? What would she say? What if they asked her lots of questions? She tried to remember what her mother had told her. Speak slowly. Look the person in the eye. Ask questions about the job. There was so much to remember. Suddenly she felt mad. It was all her mother's fault. This stupid job idea. She wished she'd never asked for that five dollars.

Jen followed her mother up the steps to the hospital. The entrance hall was cool and quiet. A nurse sat at a small desk.

"You go ahead, Jen. I'll sit down over here," Mrs. Young said.

"Can I help you?" the nurse at the desk asked.

"Uh, yes. I came to see about the job. The one that's open for the summer," Jen said.

"Your name, please?"

"Jennifer Young."

"OK. Mrs. Baxter will want to talk with you. Please take a seat. She'll be right with you," the nurse said.

Jen sat down beside her mother. She stared at the doorway and waited for Mrs. Baxter. An ambulance siren came closer and closer. Are they going to bring in somebody from a wreck, Jen wondered. She sure hoped not.

"Jennifer Young?" Someone was calling her name. A gray-haired woman was standing in the doorway.

"That's me." Jennifer stood up quickly. Her knees were shaking. Her face felt hot. There was no turning back now.

Chapter 3

Mrs. Baxter, Head Nurse

"Jennifer? I'm Mrs. Baxter, the head nurse here. I'm glad to meet you. Let's go to my office."

Jen followed Mrs. Baxter down the hall to a sunny office.

"Have a seat on the couch, Jennifer." Mrs. Baxter sat down behind her large desk. "So you're here to see about the summer job?"

"That's right. If it's still open," Jen answered.

"Have you ever had a job before?" Mrs. Baxter asked. She started writing something on a pad of paper.

"No, I haven't," Jen said. I bet I'll never get the job now, she thought.

"Well, everybody's got to start somewhere." Mrs. Baxter smiled. "As long as you're not afraid of hard work."

"Oh, no. I'm not," Jen answered quickly.

"Many of our nurses are on vacation. So we

need extra help. You'll be carrying meal trays, getting drinks for patients. You'd be busy, that's for sure." Mrs. Baxter looked over the tops of her glasses.

Doesn't sound too hard, Jen thought. Sounds like I won't have to be around any really sick or hurt people.

"The pay is four dollars an hour. You'll have half an hour for lunch. Your hours are eight until three, Monday through Friday," Mrs. Baxter said.

Twenty-four dollars a day, Jen thought. It sounded like a lot of money. One hundred and twenty dollars a week. To spend on whatever she wanted!

"That sounds great!" Jen said.

"When could you start?" Mrs. Baxter asked.

"Right away, I guess." Jen couldn't believe it. She had the job!

"Wonderful!" Mrs. Baxter stood up and put out her hand to Jen. "Welcome to Clayton General Hospital. I hope you'll like working here. I'll see you a little before eight tomorrow."

"OK, I'll be here. Thanks a lot for giving me the job," Jen said. She headed back down the hall. Suddenly she felt terrific. She had a job! She was going to earn more than a hundred

*"Welcome to Clayton Hospital.
I hope you'll like working here."*

dollars a week! She could be at the pool by three.
And the work sounded easy. No sweat. It looked
like a smooth summer ahead.

Chapter 4

Clayton General Hospital

Jen's alarm clock went off at a quarter to seven the next morning. Jen covered her head with her pillow. She was going to hate getting up so early every day. Some summer! But then she thought about getting paid on Friday and slowly sat up in bed. Her old jeans lay on the floor where she'd thrown them last night. She started to pull them on. Then she changed her mind. She took her new jeans skirt out of the closet. She'd been saving it for something special. It might as well be today. She looked at her clock and raced for the shower.

A few minutes before eight, Mrs. Young dropped Jen off in front of the hospital.

It was quiet and cool inside. Nurses were hurrying up and down the hall. Suddenly Jen felt important. She was part of all this.

Jen knocked on Mrs. Baxter's door.

"Come on in," the head nurse called.

Mrs. Baxter was talking to a tall blond girl. "Good morning, Jennifer. This is Dana Barnes. She'll be working with you this summer. Dana, this is Jennifer Young."

"Hi, Dana. Just call me Jen." Jen was surprised. She hadn't known she'd have somebody to work with.

Dana looked at Jen. "Hi," she said without smiling.

"Girls, these are your jackets. You'll wear them every day. Just slip them on over your clothes." Mrs. Baxter held up two baggy blue jackets with huge pockets.

Yuk, Jen thought. I'll look awful in that thing. Maybe I can get out of wearing it.

Dana looked at the jacket as if it were a dead snake.

"Right now I'm going to take you on a short tour of the hospital," Mrs. Baxter said. "Then we'll talk about what you'll be doing today." She walked towards the door. "And be sure to put on your jackets. You're part of the hospital now."

Jen and Dana slowly pulled on the jackets. Then they followed Mrs. Baxter down the hall.

Half an hour later Mrs. Baxter led Jen and Dana back into her office.

"We're not real busy right now. Only ten beds are full," Mrs. Baxter said. "But sometimes all thirty beds are full. That could happen at any moment. Then we're really busy. But it looks like a pretty quiet week ahead."

Dana sat down on the couch. She stretched and yawned.

"Not tired already, are you? The day's just started. There's work to be done," Mrs. Baxter said. "I want you girls to start by checking that each patient has water."

That sounds easy enough, Jen thought. Ten patients—she and Dana could each take five. They could finish up pretty quickly. Probably have lots of free time.

The loudspeaker called Mrs. Baxter's name. "I've got to go. Come find me if you have any questions." Mrs. Baxter raced off down the hall.

"Might as well get started," Jen said. "We can each take one side of the hall. OK?"

"What's the big rush? Mrs. Baxter's not going to know if we hang out here a little longer." Dana put her feet up on the couch.

"Well, I guess I'll start. See you later," Jen said. This Dana is something else, she thought. I'd better be careful. She'll have me doing all her work.

Jen walked to the first room on the hall. A pretty blond woman lay in the bed holding her baby. She smiled as Jen came in.

"Hi. Can I get you some fresh water?" Jen asked.

"No, thanks. But I'd love some juice. Could you get me some?" the woman asked.

"Sure. I'll be back in just a minute." Suddenly the baby began to scream. Jen quickly left the room. That crying drives me crazy, she thought. Good thing I didn't take that day care job.

Jen walked to the kitchen. Mrs. Baxter had shown her where the juices were kept.

Dana was standing by the refrigerator. Jen was surprised to see her there. "I thought you were down in the office," she said.

"I got thirsty," Dana said. She opened the refrigerator and took out a can of soda.

"Hey, we're not supposed to take those. They're for the patients," Jen said.

"Who's to know?" Dana snapped open the can.

Jen took a can of juice out of the refrigerator. The cans of cold soda on the shelf looked awfully good. Maybe Dana was right. No one would know if she took one. But she just didn't feel good about it.

"See you later," Dana said as Jen left the kitchen.

Suddenly Jen felt the floor start to move! It was rolling from side to side! Jen stuck her arms straight out for balance. The can of juice crashed to the floor. Walls, floor, ceiling—everything was moving! Someone screamed. Jen could make no sound when she opened her mouth. Carts rolled crazily down the hall. Bottles crashed to the floor. A huge roar sounded in Jen's ears. The shaking went on and on. And then everything went dark.

Chapter 5

Earthquake!

The roaring stopped. Everything was still. There was just blackness. Where was she? What had happened? Had a bomb fallen?

Suddenly the lights came on. Jen stared at the hallway ahead of her. It was covered with broken glass. Tables had turned over. Medicine bottles lay all over the floor. Where was everyone? Jen did not move. She looked down at her arms and legs. No cuts. She had been lucky. A window had crashed in right beside her.

Suddenly a baby started to wail. Then Jen heard a moaning sound. Where was it coming from?

"Please! Somebody!" The voice was very weak. It was coming from around the corner. Jen pulled herself to her feet. She was shaking all over. She felt dizzy—almost seasick. The hall still seemed to be going round and round. Jen started towards the sound of the scream. What if the shaking starts again, she thought. I'll fall into all this broken glass. She turned the corner of the hall. Then she stopped and stared. The body of a nurse lay on the floor. And there was a pool of blood around it. The nurse's eyes were closed. Jen kept staring at the body. She wanted to scream, too. Suddenly she heard the sound of running feet. It was Mrs. Baxter. Her white uniform was torn and spotted by blood.

"Jennifer! You're OK! Thank heaven." Mrs. Baxter hugged Jen and then knelt down to the body on the floor. "It's Sally." She pressed her fingers against Sally's neck. "Her heartbeat's still strong. Good sign. But this bleeding from the nose and ears is bad. Could mean a fractured skull. We've got to get more doctors here. But the earthquake has blocked the roads."

Earthquake! For a moment Jen forgot to breathe. An earthquake. And she had come through it. But what about her mother? Was she safe? Jen's heart pounded with fear.

"My mother! I've got to find out if she's OK," Jen cried. "She's in that highrise office building. What if it fell in the earthquake?"

Mrs. Baxter put her arm around Jen. "I bet she's safe. Don't worry. Those highrise buildings

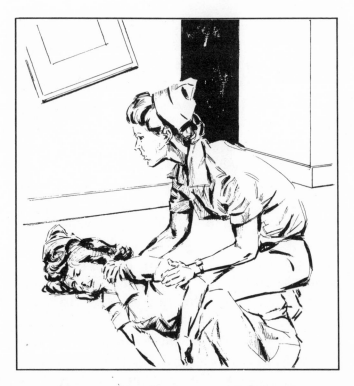

She pressed her fingers against Sally's neck.

are built to be safe in earthquakes. And your mother knows where *you* are. That's important." Mrs. Baxter began to wash away the blood from Sally's face.

"But I've got to know. I've got to find her!" Jen kept seeing her mother trapped under a huge building.

"All our phone lines are dead. The wires fell down in the earthquake. But the hospital has a CB radio. They'll try to contact your mother's office. I bet she's already at an emergency shelter. Just like Dana's family," Mrs. Baxter said.

Dana! Jen had forgotten all about her. "Dana's OK? She wasn't hurt?"

"Not a scratch. She's helping get extra beds ready right now. We have to make room for a lot of people. The ambulances will soon bring them in. But the roads are blocked. The ambulances can't get through yet."

Mrs. Baxter carefully cleaned the cuts on Sally's face. "I hope the doctor gets here soon. Just our luck—only one doctor in the hospital when the earthquake hit!"

She put a clean cloth into Jen's hand. "Here. You take over. I'll go get an oxygen tank. And we'll need a guerney to move Sally out of here. I'll be right back."

Guerney? What's a guerney, Jen thought. It must be one of those carts on wheels for moving sick people. She began to slowly wash away the blood from Sally's face. But it seemed to do no good. There was always more blood. And still no doctor came.

Chapter 6

A Search for Victims

"Jennifer! They need somebody to go with the paramedic in the ambulance. You go. I'd better stay here." Mrs. Baxter knelt down beside Sally.

Go in an ambulance? Jen couldn't believe what she was hearing. They'd be bringing in the earthquake victims. There would be blood, bodies. And she'd be right there. There'd be no escape.

"Come on! I've got the engine running!" A young red-haired man was standing by the door. "Hurry up," he said.

There wasn't time to think. Jen hurried down the hall and out the door. She climbed up onto the high front seat of the ambulance.

"I'm Sam Walters. Welcome aboard!" Sam put out his hand to Jen. "You're Jennifer? Thanks for coming along. I really needed somebody to help me out." Sam backed the ambulance out of the driveway. "I always have another paramedic

20

along. But right now none of them can get through to the hospital. Pretty bad earthquake."

"It was awful. I was so scared. I'll never forget how that shaking felt," Jen said.

"The earthquake measured 7.0 on the Richter scale. I just heard it on my radio," Sam told Jen.

"What's the Richter scale?" Jen asked.

"It's a scale that measures the strength of earthquakes," Sam said. "7.0 is a pretty strong quake. The famous San Francisco earthquake of 1906 measured 8.3. It wiped out almost the whole city."

Jen stared out at the street ahead. She couldn't believe what she was seeing. Houses sagged. Front porches had caved in. This was the town's main street. Now it was piled high with bricks and wrecked cars. Fronts of stores had fallen into the street. Were people buried under the fallen walls? Jen felt a chill go through her body.

"Look at all that smoke," Sam said. "Fires burning out of control. This town doesn't have enough fire trucks. They'll have to bring some in from other towns."

Suddenly Jen thought of something. "Sam, my mother works in that new highrise building. Did you hear if it was OK in the earthquake?" Jen held her breath.

"Yes. Don't worry. I heard about it on the CB. It held up fine. Everybody got out OK. That's a strong building." Sam drove slowly along the street. It was filled with smashed cars.

"Keep your eyes open, Jen. There might be people trapped in those cars," Sam said.

Jen stared at the smashed cars. How could anyone still be alive in one of them, she wondered. But she looked carefully into each car as they drove past.

"Sam! Wait! I think I see something. There's someone in that blue car," Jen cried.

Sam slammed on the brakes. He and Jen jumped out of the ambulance. They ran to the car. Its whole roof had been caved in by falling bricks. How could anyone still be alive inside?

"Look. On the front seat. It's a child!" Jen could see a little boy lying face down on the front seat. His back was pinned under the steering wheel. The car roof was smashed down close above his head.

Was he alive? Jen's heart pounded with fear.

Sam pulled on the door handle. It was jammed shut. "We've got to get him out of there," he shouted. He climbed up onto the hood of the car. The front windshield was shattered. Sam quickly ripped out the pieces of broken glass.

22

"Jen, I can't reach him. You'll have to lift him out. Come on up," Sam said.

Jen climbed up onto the hood of the car. She looked in at the small body jammed under the steering wheel. What if I can't get him out, she thought. How can I move him?

"OK. Here you go," Sam said. "Be careful climbing in." He helped Jen lower her legs through the windshield.

Please let him be alive, Jen thought. She touched the boy's head. Suddenly he moved. He turned his face towards her. His eyes were open. They were bright with fear and pain.

"He's alive, Sam!" Jen cried. "It's OK. We're going to get you out. Don't worry," she said to the boy. Please let me do this right, she said to herself. Don't let me hurt him.

"All right, Jen. Take hold of his shoulders. Try to slide him out from under the wheel. Very gently now. We don't know what bones might be broken," Sam said.

The roof of the car was smashed down very low. Jen could barely move. She gently took hold of the boy's shoulders. "I won't hurt you. I'm just going to move you over," she whispered. She held her breath. Could she move him? Or was he pinned too tightly under the wheel? She slowly pulled his shoulders to the side. The boy cried out with pain.

"I'm sorry. I'm sorry." Jen's hands were shaking.

"I'll pull up on the wheel while you move him. Then maybe we can get him free." Sam reached in and took hold of the wheel. "OK. Now!" he said.

Jen gently pulled again on the boy's shoulders. Sam pulled hard on the wheel. "There! He's free!" Jen cried. "We did it!"

"Great! Now let's get him out of there." Sam reached his arms in through the window. "See if you can lift him up to me."

Jen looked down at the little boy. He made no sound. He just stared up at her. His face was very white and covered with sweat. Jen knew something was very wrong. They had to work fast.

Jen braced her knees on the car seat. She bent her shoulders under the low roof. "Here he comes," she said to Sam. She put her hands under the boy's arms. Then she slowly lifted him up. The boy moaned with pain. "Just a little farther now. Just a little," Jen whispered. "There!" She felt Sam's arms take over the weight of the boy. Sam pulled him out the rest of the way. Jen climbed out right behind the boy.

"I'll get the stretcher." Sam ran to the ambulance.

Jen sat beside the boy on the hood of the car. She looked down at his small white face. "It's OK now. We're taking you to the hospital." Is he going to live, she wondered. Are his parents still alive?

Sam and Jen gently moved the boy onto the stretcher. Then they put him into the back of the ambulance.

"I'm afraid he's bleeding inside," Sam said. "He's pale, sweaty, breathing fast." Sam bent down over the boy. "Sonny, I'm going to touch your stomach real softly. Can you tell me if it hurts?"

Sam pressed down gently on the boy's stomach. The child screamed in pain. Jen felt her throat tighten up with fear. She grabbed the boy's hand.

"He's bleeding. Just like I thought." Sam gently stroked the boy's forehead. "Tell me, Sonny, does it hurt when you breathe?"

The boy nodded his head slowly. He was sweating more and more now. And breathing very fast.

"Let's get moving. There's no time to lose. I think he has a broken rib. It's torn a hole in his

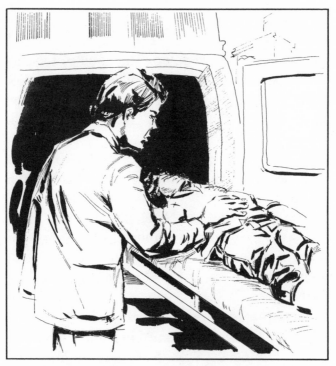

Sam pressed down gently on the boy's stomach.

lung." Sam jumped into the driver's seat. Jen knelt beside the boy in the back of the ambulance.

They raced off towards the hospital. But the roads were full of wrecked cars and fallen trees. The ambulance could only creep along. Jen's heart was pounding. They *had* to go faster. A life depended on it.

Chapter 7

Time of Fear

Sam and Jen raced to the emergency entrance of the hospital. They pushed the boy on a guerney in front of them. The hall was full of people and noise. And the walls were lined with guerneys. A person lay on each guerney. Babies cried and people moaned softly all along the hall. How can the hospital take care of them all, Jen wondered.

"Let's head for X-ray," Sam said softly. "Got to check if the rib is broken. If it has torn his lung, they'll have to operate."

Sam pushed the guerney down the hall. The boy's body looked tiny under the blanket. His eyes were wide with fear. Jen walked beside him.

They came to the door of the X-ray room.

"OK, kiddo, we'll see you later," Sam told the boy. "They're going to take some pictures of you in here."

Jen squeezed the boy's hand. "Hey—we don't

even know your name. That's pretty silly, isn't it?" She smiled. "You gonna tell us?"

The boy just stared up at her.

"Well, maybe later on. I'm Jen and this is Sam. Just so you know. See you in a little bit." Jen turned and walked away. There was a terrible tight feeling in her throat. She heard Sam talking to the X-ray nurse. She looked down at her new white sandals. They were spotted with blood. Her jacket was torn and covered with dirt. Was it only this morning that she had started work?

"Jennifer! You're back. I've got good news. Your mother's safe. She's at the emergency shelter. We let her know you're safe, too. Quick, can you help me here?" Mrs. Baxter was calling her. She was bending over a body on a guerney. "A freezer fell on this woman in the earthquake. They just brought her in. Stay with her a minute. I've got to go try to find a doctor." Mrs. Baxter put a cloth in Jen's hand. "You can clean up those cuts with this. I'll be right back." She hurried off down the hall.

The woman reached out and touched Jen's wrist. Then she smiled. Her face was streaked with blood and badly bruised. Jen began gently touching her cuts with the cloth.

"Tell me if I hurt you. I'll be very careful," Jen

said softly. Gosh, this lady's brave. I'd be screaming, she thought.

Suddenly the floor began to shake. The lights flashed off, then right back on again. People screamed. The woman on the guerney grabbed Jen's arm. Another earthquake. Jen's heart pounded. The hospital was going to fall. She was sure of it. She had to get in a doorway. Or under a table. Wasn't that what you were supposed to do? But suddenly the shaking stopped. It was over. A baby began to cry. The siren of a fire truck wailed.

Jen looked down at the woman on the guerney.

"It's OK. It's stopped. I think it was an after-shock. It didn't last long. Don't be scared." Jen smiled at the woman.

"Don't leave me!" the woman whispered.

"I won't. Don't worry," Jen was surprised how calm her own voice sounded. "What's your name?" she asked the woman.

"Katie. Katie Green. Lived here fifty years. Never had any earthquakes. Not till today."

Suddenly Dana rushed up to Jen. "I've got to get a break from this. I'm going to get a cold drink. Want to come?"

Jen stared at Dana. She couldn't believe what

Dana was doing. With all these people lying in the hallway needing help!

"Dana, you can't! Look at all these people. You can't cut out now," Jen whispered.

"Want to watch me? See you later." Dana hurried down the hall.

Jen felt hot with anger. She wanted to tell Mrs. Baxter what Dana had done. Why did Dana ever take a job here anyway? Suddenly Jen remembered something. She'd liked the idea of an easy summer job herself. Now all that seemed like a long time ago.

"Jen!" Sam rushed up. "The boy did break a rib. It tore his lung. He's going into the operating room right away. But his chances are good. The tear isn't large. He hasn't lost too much blood."

"When will we know? Oh, Sam, I'm so scared for him. And his parents. Nobody knows if they're even alive," Jen said.

"The hospital sent out a message to all the emergency shelters. If his parents are there, someone will tell them that he's here." Sam put his arm around Jen's shoulder.

"But what if they aren't at the shelter? What then, Sam? What if they're trapped somewhere or buried alive?" Jen cried.

Sam shook his head slowly. "All we can do right now is hope."

Chapter 8

Trapped!

"Jennifer!" Mrs. Baxter hurried up the hall. "Sam needs you in the ambulance again. Dana's going too. I'll take over here. The doctor's going to check on Katie. Here, Jennifer, take these sandwiches with you."

"Thanks, Mrs. Baxter." Food. She had forgotten all about it. How long had it been since she had eaten, Jen wondered. She hurried out towards the ambulance. Dana met her in the doorway.

"Why do *we* have to ride in the ambulance?" Dana asked. She looked mad. "I thought the paramedics did that."

"Because they can't get here yet. And I need your help." Sam answered Dana's question. He stood beside the ambulance. "Let's hit the road. I just heard there may be people trapped in Scott's Department Store. The whole roof may cave in at any moment."

"Scott's? I was just shopping there yesterday," Dana said. "Unreal!"

Jen felt a chill go through her body. Scott's was her favorite store. She and Julie went in there all the time. And now its roof was about to cave in!

Sam jumped into the driver's seat. The girls slid in beside him. The ambulance drove off into the night. Suddenly they could see a huge orange glow in the sky.

"Fires downtown," Sam said. "Right where we're headed. Fires do some of the worst damage in earthquakes. Whole cities can burn up. That's what happened in San Francisco in the 1906 earthquake."

Soon they could smell smoke all around them. The scream of fire sirens filled the air. They were getting close to downtown.

Suddenly Sam put on the brake. "Here's Scott's. We're lucky it hasn't caught fire yet. I'm going on in and check for people."

"Can we go in, too?" Jen asked. "We can help you."

"No. You two wait in the doorway. I'm afraid for you to come in. The roof may cave in at any minute. I'll call you if I need you. You can help me get people into the ambulance." Sam handed each girl a large flashlight. "Just in case," he said. Then he walked into the building. The girls watched his light slowly disappear in the darkness. Jen suddenly felt very much alone without Sam there. She wished they could have gone with him.

"Might as well just look inside. Gosh, what a mess!" Dana shined her flashlight into the large front room of the store. Huge chunks of concrete and plaster covered the floor. There was glass everywhere.

"That's where all the lipstick and perfume was sold," Jen said. "Look at it now." She stared in horror at the scene in front of her.

"Hey! There are boxes of stuff on the floor! Let's go see what's in them." Dana rushed into the dark room.

"Wait, Dana! Sam said not to go in there," Jen called after her.

"I'll be right back. I just want to check out these boxes," Dana yelled. "Wow! They're full of perfume bottles. And the bottles aren't broken! Here's one full of lipstick! I can't believe it."

"Dana! Remember that Sam said the building might cave in. Don't stay in there." Jen shined her flashlight into the dark room.

"Hey, cool it, Jen. I'll come when I'm ready. First I'm going to load up my pockets. I knew these jackets would be good for something! These pockets are huge."

"Dana, what are you doing?" Jen couldn't believe what Dana had said. "You can't take that perfume. That's looting. It's the same as stealing!"

"No, it's not! This stuff will all get smashed anyway when the roof falls. Why not save some of it? This is too good to pass up. Come on in. You can load up, too," Dana called to Jen.

"Dana, I mean it. Leave the stuff alone. You could get sent to jail for doing that." Jen could feel herself getting hot with anger.

"Hey, Jen, knock it off. You going to report me or something?" Dana yelled.

Jan felt an awful tightness in her chest. She knew she should report Dana for looting. Suddenly she heard a noise. It sounded like a crash, far on the other side of the store. That was where Sam had gone. A chill went through Jen's body. What was the crash? Had something happened to Sam? Should they go in and see?

"Dana, did you hear that crash? I'm scared something's happened to Sam. Come on. Let's go find him." Jen knew what she was going to do.

She was going in after Sam. There was something wrong in there in the darkness. She knew it.

Dana was coming towards Jen. "Look at this. I'm set for the year." Dana patted her full pockets. Glass bottles clinked together. "You're really missing out, Jen."

Jen didn't answer. She walked towards where the crash had come from.

"Wait up. I'm coming. Gosh, it's creepy in here." Dana followed Jen into the darkness.

Glass crunched under their feet. Jen looked up towards the roof of the store. Would it hold up? What if it came crashing down and buried them all? Don't think about it, she told herself. Just find Sam.

Jen shined her flashlight around the huge room. Suddenly she jumped back. Bodies—bodies everywhere on the floor! Heads and arms lay scattered all around. Dana screamed. Jen just stood there. She couldn't move.

"Wait. They're not real people. They're dummies, Dana. The kind stores put clothes on." Suddenly Jen felt like laughing. Boy, had they been fooled!

"I want to get out of here. This place gives me the creeps." Dana kept staring down at the dummies.

"We've got to find Sam, Dana. I know he's in here somewhere. Sam!" Jen called out his name in the darkness. "Sam, where are you?" But there was only silence.

They walked on into the next room. Jen shined her flashlight across the floor. Suddenly she saw a body. It was Sam. She knew his red hair and green jacket. His eyes blinked shut in the brightness from Jen's flashlight.

"Sam!" Jen ran over to him. Dana was close behind her. Then they saw what had happened. Jen felt a chill shoot through her body. A huge wall shelf had fallen. Sam's legs were pinned underneath it. They're crushed. I know they're crushed, Jen said to herself. She felt sick with fear.

"Sam! It's Jen and Dana." Jen knelt down beside him. His face and neck were wet with sweat. He was breathing very fast.

"Got to get it off me," Sam gasped. His voice was very weak. He's about to pass out, Jen thought. Should we run for help? That might take too long. Should we try to move the shelf ourselves? We've got to, she told herself. Sam was being crushed.

"Dana, we've got to move that shelf off him.

His face and neck were wet with sweat.
He was breathing very hard.

Get on the other side. When I count to three we'll
both lift," Jen shouted.

"Move that thing? You're crazy, Jen. We can't
do it. Let's run and get help." Dana was shivering
and staring down at Sam.

"Let's try it, Dana. We've got to try." Jen knelt
down on one side of the shelf. Dana knelt down

on the other. Perfume bottles fell out of her pockets and crashed to the floor. "OK now. Ready? One, two, three!" Jen cried. They pulled up on the shelf. "Harder! Harder!" Jen shouted. But it did not move. Were they crazy to try? Should they just run for help instead? "Once more. Let's just give it all we've got," Jen said to Dana.

Dana tore off her jacket and bent down to the shelf. "OK. Tell me when."

Once more they pulled up on the shelf. Jen felt as if her arms would break. She pulled with all her strength. "It's moving!" Dana shouted. "We've got it. Hold on!"

Jen knew she was going to let go. She just couldn't hold on any more. Her hands burned from the weight of the shelf. She felt as though her body was going to cave in with pain.

"Hang on! Step backwards," Dana cried. "We've almost got it now. We can do it. There! It's off him! Set it down easy."

Jen fell to her knees. Her whole body was shaking. Sweat poured down her face. She stared at the huge shelf. Had they really moved it?

"Jen. Dana. Thanks." Sam whispered. The girls moved close to him. "Listen. Don't move me. Go to the ambulance. Call the paramedics. I can't. . ." Sam was trying to tell them something more.

"Don't try to talk, Sam. I'll go to the ambulance. Jen, you stay here with him." Dana walked off into the darkness.

Jen looked down at Sam. His eyes were closed. Was he asleep or had he passed out? Had they not moved the shelf in time to save him? He has to make it, Jen thought. He has to. She sat there beside him in the silent darkness.

Chapter 9

Long Day's End

An hour later the paramedics were wheeling Sam into the hospital on a guerney. Jen and Dana walked beside him.

"Jennifer! Dana! We heard what you did for Sam! You're heroes!" Mrs. Baxter met the girls at the emergency room door.

"They sure are heroes," one of the paramedics said. "I don't know how they ever lifted that shelf. They saved Sam's legs. Maybe his life, too."

Jen heard what the paramedics were saying. But none of it seemed real somehow. Had it all really happened? She looked down at Sam. He was awake now. And the color had come back to his face.

"They're waiting for Sam in the X-ray room," Mrs. Baxter said. "Jennifer and Dana, come on with me. They'll let us know any news right away."

The paramedics hurried Sam off to X-ray. Jen and Dana watched them go down the hall.

"You girls must be tired and starving. Let's get you some food right away." Mrs. Baxter led Jen and Dana down to her office. They both went straight to the big couch. It felt wonderful to sit down.

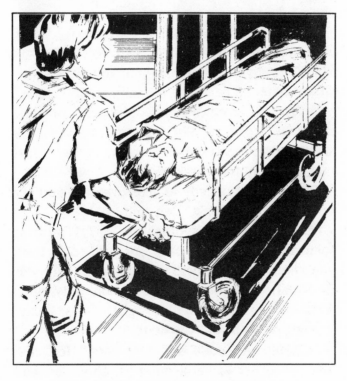

The paramedics hurried Sam off to X-ray.

"I think I'm too tired to eat," Jen said.

"Me, too." Dana leaned back against the pillows and closed her eyes.

Mrs. Baxter smiled. "Oh, Jennifer, good news on the little boy you found! He's doing fine. His lung should heal up fast. And his name's Billy King! We found his parents. They were at a shelter."

"Oh, I'm so glad! That's wonderful." Jen couldn't wait to share the news with Sam.

"We told your families where you girls were," Mrs. Baxter said. "They're really anxious to see you. The paramedics can drop you off on their next trip into town. Both your families are at a shelter. Everyone's spending the night there. Just in case of another quake."

Both girls groaned. "There *can't* be another one! There just can't," Jen said.

"Some first day on the job, eh? I promise tomorrow won't be as bad. But we'll really need you here. We have three times as many full beds as usual. I've got to get back on duty now. You've done a fine job today, girls." Mrs. Baxter waved and went out the door.

"I could just conk out right here," Jen said. She pulled her jacket around her shoulders and leaned back on the couch. "Hey, Dana, where's

42

your jacket?" she asked. Suddenly she remembered. Dana had stuffed the jacket full of lipstick and perfume.

Dana looked down at the floor. "I left it back there where we found Sam. I guess I'll have to get a new one. That was sort of a dumb thing I did—grabbing up all that stuff. I just want to forget about it."

"Me, too. Let's forget it. The main thing is that we found Sam. Boy, that shelf sure was heavy, wasn't it? You're the one that kept us going, Dana. I was sure I was going to drop it. You sure are strong!" Jen said.

"Well, I guess I didn't work as hard as you did the rest of the day. Maybe that had something to do with it." Dana smiled.

"They'll have plenty of work for both of us tomorrow. That's for sure," Jen said. She stood up and stretched. "Let's go try to catch a ride to the shelter. Gosh, it seems like about a year since I've seen Mom!"

"This morning sure seems like a long time ago. A lot has happened to us today." Dana pulled herself up from the couch.

"Do you think it'll get boring around here when the excitement is all over?" Jen asked.

"Oh, I doubt it. Mrs. Baxter would never let

that happen!"

"That's OK," Jen laughed. "After today we can handle *anything!*"